# 50

## fantastic ideas for
## circle time

FEATHERSTONE

Bloomsbury Publishing Plc
50 Bedford Square, London, WC1B 3DP, UK

A catalogue record for this book is available from the British Library

ISBN: PB: 978-1-4729-5266-0; ePDF: 978-1-4729-5265-3

2 4 6 8 10 9 7 5 3

Printed and bound in India by Replika Press Pvt. Ltd.

All papers used by Bloomsbury Publishing Plc are natural, recyclable products from wood grown
in well managed forests. The manufacturing processes conform to the environmental regulations of
the country of origin

To find out more about our authors and books visit www.bloomsbury.com and sign up for our newsletters

# Contents

# Introduction

**M**ost EYFS settings will be familiar with 'circle time' as a regular opportunity to spend time together as a group, allowing all children access to activities, shared responsibility for its outcome, and providing equal attention from practitioners as everybody can be seen and heard. Circle time is an important part of life in the EYFS. Everybody is valued. Everybody sits at the same level. Everybody can speak, or not, as they feel able.

However, I know that as practitioners we are always on the lookout for further inspiration and constantly seeking new and stimulating ways to further enrich a tried-and-tested idea.

The activities in this collection include all areas of the early years curriculum, and there are activities and games to develop children's personal, physical and communication skills alongside more focused mathematics and literacy activities and, of course, opportunities to be creative.

Most of the time, circle time will involve all of the children together, but many of these games also work well with smaller groups, especially with younger children. Encourage children to revisit games and activities independently and spontaneously. If they have enjoyed an activity and choose to initiate a group of their peers to play it again, then you know it has engaged their learning.

I also choose to involve 'talk partners' in many of the activities as this is another key part of learning in the EYFS (see Talk partner, talk, p.20). Encourage children to sit next to their current talk partner in the circle so that they can turn to them as and when the activities suggest.

Circle time works best with a few basic rules that the children all understand and are involved in creating (see Come and join us, p.6). Try the 'Big 5' rules, one for each finger on your hand, as a starter:

1.  *Listen with your ears*

2.  *Look with your eyes*

3.  *Use a quiet voice*

4.  *Keep your brain busy*

5.  *Keep your body still.*

## Useful resources

- Lolli-pot: is a fair way to choose children for an activity! Write the names of all the children onto lolly sticks and place in a pot. When you need to choose, pull out a lolly stick!

- Set of whiteboards and pens should be accessible at circle time. One for each talk partner pair is adequate. Use these different ways to signal the beginning and end of the activity depending on the ELG covered:

  Maths – 3, 2, 1, start/stop

  Literacy – A, B, C, start/stop

  PD – ready, steady, go/stop

- Bottles of calm: fill clear plastic bottles three quarters full with water, add a small bottle of clear glue (not white PVA) and shake. Add some glitter. The more glue you add the longer it takes the glitter to settle. Secure the lid and give it another shake. Optional extras include a drop of food colouring, sequins, beads, shells and tiny plastic toys.

- Squidgy feeling faces: stretch some empty balloons before filling. Make a cone out of paper and fill the balloons with two to three tablespoons of flour. Push the flour down into the balloon using a wooden spoon until it makes a solid ball. Tie a knot in the top and draw a face on the front with a permanent marker. Choose lots of different feeling faces.

## Using this book

The pages are all organised in the same way. Before you start an activity, it's important to read everything on the page. Sometimes you may decide to change the order or just pick and choose a game from the middle – that is allowed!

**What you need** lists the items needed for the activity. Don't forget to find enough space and time for a circle as a general starting point. It's important to find a big enough space so children are able to sit comfortably and aren't squashed. Include time for a circle in your daily planning. The experience shouldn't be rushed! Most other requirements are basic and will probably already be available in your setting.

**Top tips** give a brief word of advice that could make all the difference to the successful outcome of the activity, so make sure you read them!

**What to do** provides step-by-step instructions on how to play the games. There are often multiple games included in each idea, so feel free to pick and choose the ones most suitable to your requirements.

**Taking it forward** gives ideas for additional activities to challenge the children and broaden their experiences. If something goes particularly well, these activities will extend the fun even further!

**What's in it for the children?** lists some of the benefits the children will gain through the activities and how it will contribute to their learning.

**The USP** of this collection is that the ideas are organised into each of the Early Learning Goals, which makes it easy to share with parents.

# Come and join us
## Circle time rules

## What you need:

- A puppet
- Talking stick
- Whiteboards
- Cardboard, pictures and laminator

: **Top tip** ⭐

Involve the children in making the rules so that they fully accept and understand them. Have some ideas of your own ready to provide guidance.

### What's in it for the children?

The children will feel more valued, and that their views are being taken seriously, if they are involved in decisions about circle time rules.

### Taking it forward

- How many of the circle time rules can children remember at the next circle time? Point out the display to remind them.

- Try changing the words of the last line of the 'Come and join us' song to create some more verses. Relate them to the activity that you are planning for instance: *Tell a story*, *Make a shape*, *Play a drum*, and so on.

## What to do:

1. Invite the children to come and join you in a circle so that everybody can see each other. Bring the puppet along with you (see Puppet play, p.7).

2. Introduce the word 'rules'. Sometimes an activity needs rules in order for it to work properly.

3. Model somebody who isn't following the rules – calling out, waving arms around, bouncing up and down, etc. Use the puppet to role play the difference between behaving well and behaving badly.

4. Let the children take turns using the 'talking stick' (see Taking turns, p.8) to share their ideas for some rules. If their ideas are inappropriate, respond with 'thank you'. If they don't want to speak, invite them to whisper their idea to the puppet.

5. Guide them to variations of these: listening ears, looking eyes, quiet voices, thinking brain, keep body still, raise hand (finger on nose).

6. Ask the children to draw simple pictures to represent the rules.

7. Print and laminate pictures and display them clearly for children to see.

8. Sing this song to the tune of 'London's Burning':

   *Come and join us, (x2)*
   *In a circle. (x2)*
   *Sit down! (x2)*
   *Listen quietly. (x2)*

# Puppet play
## Getting to know each other

## What you need:

- A puppet (preferably with a moving mouth)
- Talking stick
- Pencils
- Paper

## Top tip ★

Only operate the puppet yourself and keep it away from the children when not in use. If you're not very confident using a puppet, practise in front of the mirror at home first!

### What's in it for the children?

Children gain in confidence as they befriend the puppet. They become more able to share problem-solving ideas and tell stories as part of a group.

### Taking it forward

- Share the puppet's backstory with the children. Involve the puppet in class and school events. Celebrate his/her birthday with the children.
- Use the puppet in problem-solving activities. After play, sit in a circle and let the children see that the puppet is feeling sad. Ask him/her to share what is making him/her sad. Perhaps nobody would play with him/her. Is he/she worried about something? Can the children suggest ways to help the puppet?

## What to do:

1. Introduce the puppet to the children and ask him/her to say hello to each of the children around the circle. Can they reply using his/her name?

2. Ask the children to tell the puppet about the rules of circle time (see Come and join us, p.6).

3. Use the 'Talking stick' (see Taking turns, p.8) to show the puppet how to take turns when talking in the circle.

4. Let the children take turns to ask the puppet questions about him/herself such as age, family, pets, favourite games, football team, etc.

5. Can they interview the puppet about recent events at school and film the conversation?

6. Play a game of 'What happens next?'. Start a story and invite the puppet to continue telling it. When the puppet stops at a suitable 'cliff hanger', ask the children to take turns to say 'what happens next'.

7. Let the children write and illustrate the story they have made up together and create a puppet storybook.

# Taking turns
## Making it fair

## What you need:

- 30 cm length of wood or a stiff cardboard tube
- Materials to decorate e.g. paint, glitter, feather, ribbons, etc.

## What to do:

1. Make a talking stick with the children. Take a 30 cm length of broom handle or a stiff cardboard tube and decorate it with any crafty materials you have available to you.

2. Invite the children to sit in a circle next to their talk partners (see Talk partner, talk, p.20).

3. Explain that you are going to play some games involving taking turns. Let the children share some of their ideas about how to choose children and make it fair.

4. Grab your stick and introduce it to the children as the 'Talking stick'. Explain that only the person holding the stick can talk while everybody else in the circle listens.

5. Pass the stick around the circle and invite children to say their name and choose their favourite colour, animal, game or song.

6. Try some 'talk partner, talk' (see p.20) and ask children to take turns with their partner to talk.

7. Try singing this simple 'taking turns' song to the tune of 'Daisy Bell (Bicycle Built for Two)':

   *My turn, your turn, waiting at circle time.*

   *My turn, your turn, lining up in the line.*

   *You really won't have to wait long,*

   *Just time to sing this new song,*

   *Taking turns, taking turns,*

   *Will make it fair for you.*

8. The 'Talking stick' can be a good way to resolve conflict between a pair or small group of children. Sit them down and remind them that they can only talk when they are holding the stick and the other children should try to listen.

## Top tip ⭐

Waiting to take your turn is very hard for some children, so have props available to help them such as teddies or 'bottles of calm' (see Introduction, p.4).

## What's in it for the children?

The children will soon learn that everybody in the circle is valued and that their time to speak will come!

## Taking it forward

- Write the children's names onto a set of lolly sticks and place them in a pot – the 'Lolli-pot' (see Introduction, p.4). Pick a stick out of the pot and read out the name. This shows the children another fair way of choosing whose turn it is next to answer a question or try out a new activity.

- Try making 'bottle of calm' for children who find it hard to wait for their turn (see Introduction, p.4).

- Use a sand timer to create a brief 'time out' for children who still struggle to wait their turn or break other rules.

# Sharing and caring

Showing consideration for others

## What you need:

- A large plastic ball
- A washable marker pen

## Top tip ★

Choose a time to share and care when both good and bad things have happened. Don't just focus on the negatives or children will associate circle time with being told off!

## What's in it for the children?

This is a classic circle time activity providing children with the opportunity to share with each other in a non-threatening environment and allowing them to be involved in initiating the choice of topic.

## Taking it forward

- Invite children to choose words or phrases to write on the ball so that the sharing is child initiated. This is a key development of circle time. What do they want to talk about today?

- Alternatively, you can use your circle time 'Teddy Talk' for this activity instead of the ball. Remind the children that they can only talk to the circle when holding the Teddy.

## What to do:

1. Make your own 'sharing and caring' ball by writing words onto a plastic ball in marker pen. Use washable pen so you can change the words to match different situations.

2. Write the words 'happy' and 'funny' if you want the children to share about things that make them laugh or feel happy.

3. If you want the children to think about how to help each other, write 'we can help' or 'just ask'.

4. Try the phrases 'I forgot' or 'we all make mistakes' to help children share things that have gone wrong or that make them upset.

5. Invite the children to sit next to their talk partners in a circle (see Talk partner, talk, p.20).

6. Show the children the ball and talk about the different words written on it.

7. Invite them to pass, roll or throw the ball around the circle. Anybody can stop, choose a word or statement, and share.

8. If children are reluctant to share, don't pressure them. Let them turn and talk to their partner instead for a moment of 'talk partner, talk' (see p.20).

# Talking to teddy
## Sharing thoughts and feelings

## What you need:

- A teddy bear or soft toy

## Top tip ⭐

This is a good activity to try at the end of a session so children can reflect on how they feel about the events of the day.

### What's in it for the children?

Some children may find it easier to express their thoughts and feelings to a close friend, talk partner or soft toy. Make Teddy available for any children who are upset during the day.

### Taking it forward

- As children become more confident with circle time, allow them to set up mini-circle time with a small group of children and invite Teddy to join. This encourages children to initiate their own opportunities to play and engage together in groups.

- Let children have photographs taken with Teddy involved in different activities. Develop his character or personality as part of your PSED work. This is different to puppet work as Teddy can be handled by the children.

## What to do:

1. Invite the children to sit in a circle next to their talk partner or a friend they are happy to share with (see Talk partner, talk, p.20).

2. Introduce Teddy or a soft toy to the group. Share his/her name or choose a name together.

3. Talk about how Teddy likes to be passed carefully around the circle, not thrown!

4. Start by saying that Teddy is feeling sad. Give a reason such as 'he's feeling left out', 'he's lonely because his friend isn't here' or 'he's worried about something'.

5. Tell children that they are going to try and cheer him up. Can they talk to Teddy as he moves around the circle? If they cannot think of anything to say, just give him a hug.

6. Ask the children if any of them have problems similar to Teddy. Would they like to talk to Teddy and share their thoughts or feelings?

7. Try to relate the activity to experiences the children may have had during their day or specific events that have happened.

# What's in a name?

A good way to learn names

## What you need:

- A small drum or tambourine
- A list of the children's names

## Top tip ⭐

If a child is too shy to join in on their own, let them pass the drum to their neighbour.

## What to do:

1. Start with a small group of children and tell them you are going to play a name game. Invite the puppet to join the game (see Puppet play, p.7).

2. Tap the drum two times and then count 'one, two' aloud. Invite the children to join in with the drum by tapping on their knees.

3. Ask them to count 'one, two' using their 'thinking voice', e.g. silently in their heads.

4. Say your name in the gap created by the 'one, two' and invite the children to take turns saying their name in subsequent gaps. Can everybody fit their name in the gap?

5. As you play, other children will start watching and want to join in. Invite them to sit in the circle until the whole class is involved.

6. Show the children how to tap the rhythm of their name on the drum as you say it out loud. Point out that some will have short names and only require one tap, while others will have three or four taps.

7. Explain that you are going to pass the drum around the circle. Keep tapping two times on the knees in-between each name.

8. Ask the children to tap the rhythm of their name on the drum when it's their turn.

## What's in it for the children?

Learning everybody's name at the start of term is a challenge children will enjoy tackling by playing this game. The first step to making friends is learning something about each other.

## Taking it forward

- Can the children think of a way to make the gaps longer? Try tapping three or four times and counting aloud as you do so.

- If you have enough instruments, try giving the children a drum or tambourine each to tap the repeated rhythms on. Try some other drum circle activities. Ask all the children to place the drums on the floor in front of them. Use simple start and stop signals to encourage children to follow instructions. Invite a child to take on the role of conductor, stopping and starting the drums.

- Change the game so the children must say different things in the gaps such as favourite animals or food. Challenge the children to try not to repeat a word that has gone before!

# The singing circle

Start the day singing with friends

## What you need:

- A list of the children's names

## Top tip ⭐

Don't worry about your singing voice. It will sound great to the children as long as you act confidently!

### What's in it for the children?

Children gain confidence in using their voice in different ways including singing in a non-threatening environment. They can learn each other's names and get to know each other better.

### Taking it forward

- Invite a confident child to sing 'Where is _____ sitting today?' for you. Ask the children if they can think of a new response to the question, such as 'Over here, sitting by the window' or 'Here I am, look at my new shoes'. Take care as this extends the activity into 'show and tell' and can take up more time.

## What to do:

1. Invite the children to sit in a circle on the floor. Make sure they all have enough room and nobody is squashed.

2. Explain that you are going to take the register in a new way today – by singing their names. This is a great way for you and the children to learn each other's names at the start of a new year.

3. Demonstrate by singing to a confident child, 'Where is (child's name) sitting today?'. Any tune will do but using the two-notes from a 'cuckoo' call seems to work well.

4. The response from the child is 'Here I am' accompanied by a wave.

5. Start the register by singing to each child and waiting for their response. Reluctant singers can say the words or just wave to start with. Praise children who are brave enough to sing back to you.

6. When the children are more confident, add another line to the response and help them to learn the names of the other children. Can they see who is sitting near them and sing, 'Here I am, sitting next to (child's name)'?

# Greetings to all

**Different ways to greet each other**

## What you need:

- A list of greeting words in different languages

## Top tip ⭐

Introduce a new EAL puppet for this activity who speaks a different language, preferably one understood by one or more of the children.

**What's in it for the children?**

This is a good way to get to know each other at the start of a term or session and to include EAL children's home languages in your play. Children will enjoy using the simple rhyme to dramatic effect.

**Taking it forward**

- Display some of the greetings in different home languages around the setting so children can use them and share them with their families.

- This activity also works with the 'Tommy Thumb' rhyme.

- If you have a child or teacher in your setting who is deaf or hard of hearing, learn some simple sign language to greet them.

## What to do:

1. Start the circle time by singing each child's name and inviting them to come and sit in the circle. Or sing 'Come and join us' (see p.6).

2. Invite the children to turn to their neighbour, on both sides, and say 'hello'.

3. Can the children think of any other ways to say hello or greet each other? Encourage them to smile, wave, high five or hug.

4. Say the 'Two Fat Gentlemen Met in a Lane' finger rhyme.

5. Ask for two children to go into the middle of the circle, bow to each other and say 'How do you do?'.

6. They can choose which character to be from the rhyme – fat gentlemen, thin ladies, tall policemen, naughty school children or babies.

7. Encourage them to get in character. How will their body language change? What other actions or greetings could they use?

8. Use the 'Lolli-pot' (see Introduction, p.4) to choose more pairs to have a go at greeting each other in different dramatic ways inside the circle.

9. Try some greetings in different languages using some of the children in your group's home languages.

# Throw that feeling

A cooling down game

## What you need:

- A beanbag animal

## What to do:

1. Invite the children to sit in a circle so that they can see everybody in the group.

2. Talk about different feelings. Ask children to identify feelings from facial expressions using emojis, toys, drawing pictures or by pulling faces.

3. Try this drama game. Introduce the beanbag animal to the group and explain that it likes to share its feelings.

4. Choose a child to throw the beanbag to and shout out a feeling as you do, e.g. happy, sad, angry, tired, scared, worried, excited, proud, embarrassed, etc.

5. The catcher must try and pull a face to match the feeling. Then they can choose the next person, throw the beanbag and shout out a different feeling.

6. Finish by 'Passing a smile' around the circle. Turn to the child next to you, smile at them, and ask them to pass it on.

7. Can the smile make it all the way round the circle before it's time to go home?

### Top tip ⭐

This is a good activity for the end of the day – for cheering up, winding down and saying goodbye.

### What's in it for the children?

Children will develop more understanding of feelings by reading facial expressions. This will help them to be more aware of their own and each other's feelings.

### Taking it forward

- Buy or make your own 'squidgy feeling faces' for the children to handle during circle time (see Introduction, p.4). Can the children change the expression on their balloon face just by squashing and stretching it?

- These are also effective anti-stress balls. Encourage children to share what makes them feel stressed or worried.

# Active listening
## Listening to stories

## What you need:

- Sheets of paper with an asterisk printed on them
- Straws or lolly sticks
- Storybooks
- Props and small world figures related to the story

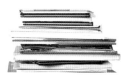

## Top tip ⭐

Children will become more effective listeners if they have a role to play during the story. Choose stories with repeated refrains.

### What's in it for the children?

Children enjoy listening out for names and objects so they can interact with the storyteller and become active listeners.

### Taking it forward

- Try some other listening games involving word rhythms. 'Echo clapping' – ask children to copy simple rhythm patterns that you clap (see Rhythm games, p.63). 'Character clap' – choose a character from a story or rhyme and say and clap their name as a word rhythm, for instance Rumpelstiltskin, Goldilocks, Humpty Dumpty, etc., for the children to copy. Let them take turns at leading the game.
- Listen and watch while the children take turns to make up their own stories using the props.

## What to do:

1. Create flags by printing asterisks on sheets of paper and sticking straws or lolly sticks to them to form the pole.

2. Ask children to sit in a circle next to their talk partner.

3. Place lots of familiar story and picture books in the middle for children to enjoy. Invite each pair to choose a book to share together.

4. Choose a pair to share their book with the circle. Make sure all the children know the story well.

5. Try acting out the story 'in the round'.

6. Choose a nursery rhyme or one of the favourite stories to retell but make some 'mistakes' for the children to correct. Explain that they should wave their asterisk flag when they hear a mistake.

7. Encourage active listening by giving some children props or small world figures represented in the story. Invite them to lift their toy into the air each time their prop is mentioned in the story.

# Let's tell a story
Make up a story together

## What you need:

- A smooth stone that fits into the palm of a child's hand – the 'story stone'
- Containers with lids filled with lots of small items to inspire storytelling – the 'storytelling tin'

## Top tip ⭐

Change the contents of the story tin regularly so children are constantly surprised and inspired to make up new stories. Practise telling stories yourself without a book to rely on.

## What to do:

1. Sing 'Come and join us' (see p.6) and change the last line to *Tell a story* as the children gather in the circle.

2. Show the children the 'story stone' and explain how it works. The stone is passed around the circle and whoever is holding it can add the next part to the story.

3. Reassure children that if they cannot think of anything to say, the 'story stone' can be passed on.

4. Start by retelling a story that is familiar to the children, either a traditional story or a storybook that you have recently shared.

5. Challenge them to think of alternative endings to the story.

6. Explain that the 'story stone' now wants to create a brand-new story. Use conventional story starters such as 'Once upon a time' and let children think of new characters.

7. Encourage children to think of an interesting setting for the story.

8. Introduce the 'storytelling tin' as a resource full of story prompts to guide the story. The items can relate to a book you are reading or be more open to interpretation and allow children to use their imagination.

9. Here are some ideas for creating stories with items to stimulate children's imagination:

   *Under the sea*: mermaid peg dolls, shells, dried sea weed or coral, plastic fish and other sea creatures, e.g. shark, octopus.

   *Pirates*: eye-patch, treasure, hook, scarf, toy boat, plastic shark, etc.

   *Knights, dragons and castles*: helmet, sword, shield, toy horse, dragon, etc.

   *Fairies in the forest*: fairy wings, wand, leaves, stones, toadstool, magic rings, etc.

   *Animals*: toy plastic animals, soft toys, animal food, etc.

10. Children can select an item from the tin to include in the story if they wish.

### What's in it for the children?

Children enjoy sharing their ideas for stories with each other. Circle time offers a non-threatening environment and removes the immediate pressure of having to write it all down!

### Taking it forward

- Invite children to act out the story that the circle has created and use some drama ideas.

- Allow children access to the 'storytelling tins' for small group work. Invite them to use the items for small world play, to make up stories and then retell them to the group.

- Let children create their own 'storytelling tin' to share at the next 'Let's tell a story' circle time with items of their own choice inside.

50 fantastic ideas for circle time

# Talk partner, talk
## Chatting with a friend

## What you need:

- A photo of each child
- Board
- Sticky tack
- Talking stick

### Top tip ★

Try to change the talk partners each week so that children have lots of opportunities to talk to different children. Some partnerships will be more successful than others!

### What's in it for the children?

Talking to one child, i.e. their talk partner, is a lot less daunting for some children than speaking to the whole group. It's also a good way for children to get to know each other and become more aware of each other's feelings.

### Taking it forward

- Let children know that they can talk to you if they are having a problem with their talk partner, such as they won't talk or don't allow them to talk. It's a practice that has to be practised.

- Use 'talk partner, talk' as a style of questioning in lots of different circle time activities.

## What to do:

1. Explain to children that you are going to choose a friend or partner for them to talk to during the 'talk partner, talk' circle.

2. Reassure them that this is a random selection and use the 'Lolli-pot' to choose each pair (see Introduction, p.4). If the number of children isn't even, use some 'talking trios'.

3. Create a talk partner board by sticking the children's photos onto a board with sticky tack so they can refer to it later.

4. Ask the children to sit in a circle next to their talk partner.

5. Invite children to find out one interesting fact about their partner, for instance favourite colour, game, book, school activity, etc.

6. Ask the children to take it in turns to tell the circle what they have learned about their partner. Use the 'Talking stick' or another object passed around the circle (see Taking turns, p.8).

7. Test how well children are listening by asking questions. What was Zach's favourite colour? Or how many children liked playing football?

# Wonderful words

Enjoy playing with words

## What you need:

- Word of the week card
- A recording of 'Sing after me' or similar echo songs

## Top tip

Use a word calendar to help you think of new words to share with the children. Always demonstrate the meaning of a word by using it in a sentence.

### What's in it for the children?

This activity will extend children's vocabulary and increase their confidence in speaking together and individually.

### Taking it forward

- Try some other word games. 'Word pairs' – can the children think of the word that is paired with 'cup' (saucer). Try hammer/nail, lock/key, salt/pepper, etc.

- 'Opposites' – challenge two children to stand up in the circle and see which of them can say the opposite word to big, hot, high, sit, loud, fat, happy, etc.

## What to do:

1. Sit in a circle and invite children to copy what you do. Start with some simple clapping patterns, add other actions, and go onto singing/chanting words – hello, smiley face, sunny day, come and play, sit down, listen now.

2. Sing some echo songs such as 'I hear thunder', 'Boom chicka boom' or 'Sing after me'.

3. Play the 'Alliteration game'. Say a word starting with one letter and go round the circle inviting each child to add a word that starts with the same letter.

4. Play 'Word association'. Start by saying a word, e.g. 'dog', followed by three claps. The next child says the first word they can think of that is connected to that word, e.g. 'bone', followed by three claps. How long can they keep going?

5. Introduce the 'Word of the week' (WOW). Pass the new word around the circle. Make sure all the children understand what it means.

6. Try some more challenging WOW words like 'wonderful', 'immaculate', 'imagination', 'patient', etc.

7. Tell a story with a repeated refrain such as *The Gingerbread Man* or *The Three Little Pigs*. Encourage all the children to join in the refrains.

# A topic of conversation

Chatting together

## What you need:

- Cards with topics written on them
- Rubber chicken or soft toy
- Chat chair
- Plastic microphone

## Top tip ⭐

Try to differentiate when choosing tasks for different children. Challenge chatty ones to listen more, or be the interviewer, and quiet children to start by sharing with their talk partner.

### What's in it for the children?

There are lots of opportunities for children to chat on their own, to a partner and in front of an audience.

### Taking it forward

- Record some of the children in the 'Chat chair' or being interviewed. Challenge them by adding some of the rules from 'Just a minute', i.e. no repetition, hesitation or deviation!

## What to do:

1. Invite the children to sit next to their talk partners in the circle (see Talk partner, talk, p.20).

2. Start with a game of 'Categories'. Choose a category or topic and go round the circle asking each child to name an item that fits. Try animals, insects, chocolate bars, colours, etc. Explain that they aren't allowed to repeat an idea.

3. Change the game to 'Chicken run'. Choose a 'speaker' to go in the middle using the 'Lolli-pot' (see Introduction, p.4). They must name as many items in the chosen category before the rubber chicken or soft toy completes a circuit!

4. Invite the talk partners to choose a topic of conversation and chat to each other. Topics might include: at the weekend, my favourite TV programme/book/game, my family, exciting news, etc. Ask for volunteers to come out and model their conversation for the circle.

5. Introduce the 'Chat chair' and ask for a child to come out and try to talk for as long as they can on a chosen topic.

6. Add an interviewer who can ask questions to extend the conversation and, of course, use the microphone.

50 fantastic ideas for circle time

# Rolling roles

Whose role is it anyway?

## What you need:

- A variety of hats – pirate, crown, police officer, cowboy, firefighter, biker, chef, baseball cap, woolly hat, beret, sunhat, flowery hat, etc.

## What to do:

1. Sit in a circle and sing the song 'My Hat, It Has Three Corners'. Add the actions.

2. Let the children look at and try on the different hats. Explain that some of them are for specific roles while others can be worn by several different characters.

3. Try going into role as a character by wearing a particular hat. Talk to the children in character using appropriate language. Invite them to respond.

4. Ask for a volunteer to choose a hat and go into role as the character. Play 'Pass the hat'. Choose a hat to pass around the circle as you sing these words to the tune of 'London Bridge':

   *Pass the hat round the ring, round the ring, round the ring,*

   *Pass the hat round the ring, what will you say?*

5. Ask children to sit next to their talk partner and choose a pair of hats to wear. What might the two characters say to each other?

6. Develop this into a group drama inside the circle involving more children wearing hats. Add more dressing up clothes and props.

## Top tip ⭐

If children are reluctant to speak in a big group, this game also works in a small circle group which might be less threatening.

### What's in it for the children?

Drama, using mime and spoken word, is a great way to help children communicate and use their imagination.

### Taking it forward

- Try a game of 'What's my line?'. Children take turns to stand in the middle of the circle and mime doing a job such as sweeping, teaching, nursing, driving, and so on, for the others to guess.

# I think it's a...

Exploring imagination and improvisation

## What you need:

- Basic props to pass round the circle, e.g. cardboard tube, saucepan lid, piece of string, empty box, small hoop, etc.
- Balloons and marker pens

## Top tip ⭐

Remember there is no right or wrong answer in this game. Just encourage children to have a go without judgement.

### What's in it for the children?

Children enjoy using their imagination to play pretend games and communicate through mime and speaking using objects and characters.

### Taking it forward

- Invite children to work with a partner or in small groups and create a drama using two characters and two props. Use the circle as a stage and produce a play 'in the round'.

- Play 'Kim's game' with a selection of small items on a tray. Let children look at them for one minute. Then take one away and see if the children can tell you what is missing. Repeat but this time they must say what is missing by describing how to use the item but not actually naming it!

## What to do:

1. Invite the children to come and sit in a circle; a small group will work well.

2. Explain that you are going to play 'I think it's a...', the game in which children take turns to mime using a prop and others say what it is.

3. Pass a prop or object around the circle and allow the children's imaginations to get to work.

4. A cardboard tube could become a hairbrush, pencil, recorder, spoon, sword, telescope – it will become obvious as the children 'use' it. A saucepan lid could become a plate, shield, hat, frying pan, cymbal, etc.

5. Develop the game by asking the children to think of a line they could say while using the prop.

6. Blow up some balloons and draw faces on them showing feelings. Invite a child to choose a balloon and talk to it.

7. Can they make up a name and character for their balloon? Invite them to introduce their balloon character to the circle.

# Pass it on

Passing actions round the circle

## What you need:

- Large ball
- Marker pen
- Different-sized balls
- Drum

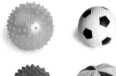

## Top tip ⭐

Make sure the children know who the leader is or you'll find lots of different actions being copied at the same time!

### What's in it for the children?

This game will develop physical control and coordination as children copy and pass on a variety of actions, changing speed and direction.

### Taking it forward

- Try a game of 'Body2body'. Call out a part of the body and ask children to join together round the circle by touching fingers, thumbs, toes, elbows, knees, and so on.

## What to do:

1. Sit in a circle so that everybody can see you and each other.

2. Draw a smiley face on a large ball.

3. Ask the children to pass the smiley ball round the circle, taking care not to drop it. Can they smile too?

4. Try the activity with different-sized balls. How quickly can they pass them all the way round? What happens when two or more balls are being passed in different directions?

5. Pass different actions around the circle. Start by asking all the children to hold hands with their neighbour. Gently squeeze the hand of the child next to you and ask them to pass it on.

6. Pass a clap round the circle. Can the children pass it in time to the beat of a drum? Try passing the clap quickly and slowly by changing the tempo.

7. Choose another signal so the clap has to suddenly change direction and go the other way round the circle.

8. Invent a sequence of moves to pass round the circle such as a clap, a wave, and a click. Change the speed and direction.

9. Invite children to make up their own sequence of moves to pass on. Remind the leader to change the speed and direction.

10. Try standing up and passing on bigger moves such as jumps, hops, bends and stamps.

# Warm up wiggles

Warm up exercises in a circle

## What you need:

- An imagination!

## Top tip ⭐

There are lots of different ways to warm up or welcome children to circle time. Establish your own routine so children recognise the format and feel safe and ready to learn.

## What to do:

1. Ask the children to sit in a circle so that they can all see you and each other. Talk about why it's important to warm up your bodies before taking exercise.

2. Try some finger rhymes such as 'I've got ten little fingers', 'Open, shut them', 'Tommy thumb', and 'Here is the beehive'.

3. Start the warm up by wiggling all your fingers in front of you. Then teach the warm up wiggles rhyme as the children copy each action.

4. *Wiggle your fingers in the air,*
   *Wiggle your fingers everywhere.*

   *Flash your fingers in the sky,*
   *Flash your fingers very high.*

   *Shake your hands to the side,*
   *Shake your hands and make them hide.*

   *Float your hands up and down,*
   *Float your hands to the ground.*

   *Shrug your shoulders up and down,*
   *Shrug your shoulders round and round.*

   *Twist at the hips and turn to the side,*
   *Twist at the hips and make them glide.*

   *Bend at the knee, 1, 2, 3,*
   *Bend at the knee just like me.*

   *Touch your toes if you can,*
   *Touch your toes, that's the plan.*

   *Warm up wiggles now are done,*
   *Warm up wiggles are such fun.*

5. Invite children to lead the warm up by thinking of their own movements for everybody to copy. Play 'All change please': walk around the circle and tap a child on the shoulder. Ask them to start an action for children to copy. Tap a different child who has to change the action, and so on.

6. Warm up voices too by asking children to add a vocal sound or word to the action in 'All change please'.

### What's in it for the children?

Children will learn to recognise the importance of regular physical exercise as part of keeping healthy and that it can all start by just wiggling your fingers and toes!

### Taking it forward

- Try a game of 'Crossing the circle'. Go round the circle and number the children 1, 2, 3, 1, 2, 3, etc. Give instructions for all the number 2s to cross the circle like a ballerina/footballer/cowboy/old lady/fashion model, etc. Ask the number 1s to cross the circle as if they were a panther/snake/elephant/dragonfly/penguin, etc. Number 3s should be stuck in the mud/an icy day/walking on the moon/floating in space, etc.

- Make a display board of different well-known finger rhymes for children to select from for a rhyming warm up.

# Animal farm
Following my leader

## What you need:

- A tray
- Small world animals
- Pictures of animals
- A blank dice with plastic pockets

## Top tip ⭐

Don't be too prescriptive. Let children come up with some ideas of their own for actions and demonstrate them to the circle.

### What's in it for the children?

Imitating the sounds and movements of animals will increase their self-confidence and their control and coordination skills.

### Taking it forward

- Play 'Kim's game' by taking away one of the small world animals from the tray and asking the children to identify the missing animal by making its sound or movement.

- Try 'Simon says', e.g. 'Simon says bark like a dog', 'Simon says move like a snake'. Remind the children to move only when the instruction is preceded by the words 'Simon says'.

## What to do:

1. Sit in a circle and make sure children have got room to move on the spot.

2. Play 'Pass the growl' by choosing any animal sound to pass around the circle. Try farm animals, wild animals or pets.

3. Place a tray of small world animals in the middle of the circle. Take turns to choose an animal, imitate its sound or movement, or make up their own 'animal action' and ask all the children to follow the leader.

4. Play 'Animal farm'. Choose some agreed movements to represent each animal, for instance: dog – licking, panting, chasing tail; pig – roll on the ground; penguin – hands down by the side, turned out and waddling; elephant – use one arm as a swinging trunk; frog – squat down on all fours and jump up and down; monkey – scratching, swinging from one arm; snake – hands together, sliding into the air; crocodile – turn hands into snapping jaws; bird – flapping wings.

5. Hold up pictures of animals for the children to imitate on the spot.

6. Play 'Animal dice': slot pictures of six different animals into the dice. Roll the dice and ask everybody to imitate the animal that's shown.

7. Change one of the pictures on the dice to a question mark and let the children choose which animal to imitate.

# Up, up and away
## Moving mini-balloons

## What you need:

- A square of fabric
- Lots of different coloured balloons

## Top tip ⭐

Blow up the balloons beforehand to the size of a large orange.

### What's in it for the children?

Making the balloons move in different ways is an exciting part of this activity. It also strengthens the shoulders and upper arms and demands a high level of coordination and concentration.

### Taking it forward

- Include the colours of the balloons in the song, e.g. four red balloons or two blue balloons, etc. Look out for opportunities to practise number skills during this activity. Try making some simple number sentences. How many balloons are there altogether?

- Listen to the song 'Up up and away' by The Fifth Dimension. Play the song as the children move the balloons up and down on the fabric.

## What to do:

1. In small groups, let the children handle the mini balloons. Compare their sizes, talk about colours, and share ideas for how to make them move.

2. Sit all the children in a circle and make sure everyone has room to sit comfortably.

3. Roll out the fabric and show children how to hold onto the edges securely.

4. Practise moving the fabric slowly up and down. Explain that the children need to coordinate their movements. Can they feel the breeze as the fabric floats up and down?

5. Place one balloon in the middle of the fabric. Try singing this song to the tune of 'Skip to My Lou':

   *One balloon, bouncing around, (x3)*

   *Called for a friend to join in.*

6. Add more balloons, one at a time, and change the words of the song.

7. Give each child a balloon and let them all throw their balloons onto the material at the same time. Change the words of the song to:

   *Lots of balloons, bouncing around, (x3)*

   *All of their friends have joined in.*

# Parachute games
Moving together

## What you need:

- Parachute
- Plastic coloured balls
- Music
- Pairs of socks
- Treasure

**Top tip** ⭐

Many of these parachute games will work with a small group and a sari if a parachute isn't available.

## What to do:

1. Ask the children to sit or kneel in a circle and hold either a handle or the edge of the parachute.

2. Start by gently moving the parachute up and down together, making waves. This requires a lot of coordination and practice. Then try these parachute games.

3. **Rollerball** – Roll some balls onto the parachute and try to get them to fall through the central hole. Add a scoring system related to the different coloured balls.

4. **Popcorn** – Try to bounce the balls off the parachute like a giant pan of popcorn! Add music as they play, e.g. 'Popcorn' by Hot Butter.

5. **Merry-go-round** – Ask children to stand up, turn their bodies sideways and hold the handles or edges of the parachute with one hand. Walk around in a circle. Change direction. Try skipping, hopping and jumping!

6. **Washing machine** – Place some paired socks onto the parachute. Ask the children to stand up, turn sideways and walk around in a circle. Shout out 'faster' and 'slower' and change direction. Tumble dry the socks by bouncing them gently up and down on the parachute.

7. **Treasure hunt** – Place some 'treasure' under the parachute and invite 'divers' to run under and retrieve them before the parachute falls.

8. **Swapsies** – Ask the children to lift the parachute high into the air. Call out two children's names. They have to run under the parachute and swap places before it falls down. Change to 'Shake hands' and the two children have to shake hands under the parachute and then run back to their place!

9. **Fruit salad** – Go round the circle naming the children after three or four different types of fruit. Ask children to stand and shake the parachute. When they hear their fruit called out, the parachute must be lifted high while the named fruit run under and swap places. 'Fruit salad' means all the children must swap places at the same time!

### What's in it for the children?

The children must work together cooperatively to make the parachute games work. They also develop upper body strength by moving and manipulating the parachute.

### Taking it forward

- Ask the children to come up with some ideas for their own parachute games.

- Go outside on a sunny day and try some parachute games. The parachute will move in a different way outside. 'Mushroom' – pull the parachute taut, lower it to the ground and then raise into the air so it creates a giant mushroom. Take a couple of steps forwards and then let go!

- Create a 'Circus tent' by lifting the parachute high into the air and taking three or four steps forward into the middle. Keep holding on and then sit on the edge of the parachute. How long does the tent stay up?

50 fantastic ideas for circle time

# Quiet as a mouse

Moving without making a sound

## What you need:

- A selection of different musical instruments, enough for one per child
- A mouse finger puppet
- Paper
- Stapler
- Felt-tip pens

## What to do:

1. Invite all the children to sit in a circle and make sure they can all see you and each other.

2. Place a selection of musical instruments in the middle of the circle. Arrange them in a random pile with some balanced on top of others.

3. Choose one instrument to pass around the circle. The challenge is that it has to make it all the way around the circle without making a sound. Jingle bells or maracas work well!

4. Introduce the mouse finger puppet. Pass the puppet around the circle as you sing this song to the tune of 'Three Blind Mice':

   *Quiet as a mouse, (x2)*

   *Sitting in his house, (x2)*

   *Can you choose a sound to make?*

   *Careful of which one you take!*

   *Quiet as a mouse!*

5. Whoever is holding the mouse at the end of the song has to go into the middle of the circle and choose an instrument from the pile.

6. Can they pick up the instrument without making a sound? If they make a sound, they must replace the instrument and go back to their place.

## Top tip ★

Allow the children some time to explore the musical instruments and how they produce sound before trying this activity.

### What's in it for the children?

This is a fun game to develop control and coordination while making music quietly together! Making and using finger puppets will require lots of fine motor dexterity.

### Taking it forward

- Make finger mouse puppets with the children. Show them how to make a single cone out of a semi-circle of white paper. Staple it closed and attach two round ears. Draw a face and whiskers. Let children make their finger mice squeak, talk, sing and interact with each other.

# Remote control aerobics
## Moving in different ways

## What you need:

- **A remote control**

## Top tip ⭐

If there are too many children in the circle to exercise at the same time, put the children into groups. Let the first group exercise and then return to their seats ready to observe the next group's turn.

### What's in it for the children?

These games will help children to move confidently in lots of different ways and to negotiate the space around them safely.

### Taking it forward

- Play 'Who's in control?'. Choose one child to be 'it' and leave the circle so he/she cannot see or hear the rest of the group. Choose a 'remote controller' who everybody has to copy. Invite 'it' to return and try to identify who is the remote controller.

- Try some yoga in the circle to wind down at the end of the session. Try the 'happy baby' pose – lie on your back and hold each foot with the corresponding hand. Then move into the 'child' pose (rest position) – kneel down, stretch your hands forward and rest your forehead on floor.

## What to do:

1. Sit in a circle so that all the children can see you and each other.

2. Make a list of different things that need a remote control – TV, DVD or CD player, and other household items, toy planes and cars, etc.

3. Talk about the buttons on a remote control – start, stop, pause, fast forward, rewind, etc.

4. Try some aerobics exercises and each button pressed on the remote control will stop, start, pause, fast forward or rewind the action.

5. Introduce the menu button. Ask children to suggest different actions for the menu: jump up and down, spin on the spot, hop on one foot ten times, wave arms in the air, touch toes, pretend to sit on a chair five times, show off your muscles, balance on one leg for a count of ten, etc.

6. Take turns at being the leader or the 'remote controller'. Select an action and shout out the buttons!

7. Introduce the change channel button so children can change to a new action.

8. Remind them to change speed – going faster and slower. Which is harder?

# Mirror moves
Copying every move you make

## What you need:

- **Hand-held mirrors**

## Top tip ⭐

Create two circles by asking children to work with their talk partner and number each other 'one' and 'two'. All the number ones will make the outer circle and the number twos will be the inner circle.

### What's in it for the children?

Children learn a lot from observing and copying. This activity will encourage them to read and empathise with facial expressions and develop their physical coordination skills.

### Taking it forward

- Give the children specific actions to mime and copy in their mirror, e.g. eating a bowl of spaghetti, an apple or a packet of crisps; brushing hair, teeth, or having a haircut; opening or wrapping a present.

- Try playing 'Chain reaction'. Ask the children to stand up in the circle and turn to face the back of the person to their left. The leader starts to mime an action or way of moving. The child behind copies and then it gets passed along the chain. Does the mime stay the same all the way round the circle?

## What to do:

1. Ask the children to sit in a circle next to their talk partner (see Talk partner, talk, p.20).

2. Provide each pair of children with a hand-held mirror.

3. Ask them to look in the mirror and pull faces or make movements. What does their reflection in the mirror do?

4. Ask them to create an outer and inner circle with their partners (see Top tip). The inner circle is going to be the mirror. The outer circle is going to pull faces for their partner to copy.

5. Start with different feelings such as happy, sad, angry, tired, confused, scared or excited. Can the mirror copy their subject exactly? Ask the children to swap roles and play again.

6. Invite the children to make bigger movements for their 'mirror' to copy such as waving, clapping, tapping, stretching, stamping, jumping, etc.

7. Can they devise and perform a sequence of repeated movements for their 'mirror' to copy?

# Alphabet shopping

Playing games with initial letters

## What you need:

- Chalk or masking tape
- Letter cards

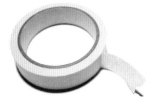

## Top tip ⭐

You can agree to 'pass' on some of the tricky letters such as q, x and z.

### What's in it for the children?

Playing word games with initial letters will increase their facility with phonics, ready for reading and writing activities.

### Taking it forward

- Try adding some alliteration so the children can use adjectives too. For instance, 'I went to the shops for an amazing apron'.

- Challenge the children's memory by seeing how many different items they can remember from the game.

## What to do:

1. Use chalk or masking tape (or alphabet cards) to make a large circle of letters of the alphabet in order.

2. Invite children to sit in the circle behind one of the letters. Letters can be shared if you have more than 26 children.

3. Play 'Alphabet shopping'. The child sitting by 'a' starts by naming an item that starts with the initial sound 'a', e.g. 'I went to the shops for an arrow'. The child behind 'b' says a word starting with 'b', e.g. 'I went to the shops for a ball', and so on.

4. Allow children to 'phone a friend' if they get stuck.

5. Change the theme of the game. Try 'the animal alphabet' and say 'I would like an "alligator" for a pet'. Go round the circle in the usual way.

6. Or try food – 'I like to eat "apples" for lunch'.

7. Play a game of 'Alphabet soup'. Put a pot of magnetic or plastic letters in the middle of the circle. Use the 'Lolli-pot' (see Introduction, p.4) to choose a child to come and give it a stir, pick out a letter, say it, and think of a word that begins with the same letter. Can they find the child in the circle who is sitting by the matching letter?

# The name game

What's in a name?

## What you need:

- Puppet
- A list of the children's names
- Strips of paper and pencils
- Scissors and glue
- Coloured strips of card

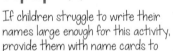

## Top tip ⭐

If children struggle to write their names large enough for this activity, provide them with name cards to trace.

### What's in it for the children?

This is a great cross-curricular activity with opportunities to practise writing their name, handling scissors and counting.

### Taking it forward

- Record the information on a chart to display on the wall. Try to stick all the four-letter names on one colour and all the five-letter names on a different colour, and so on.

- Choose other special words to experience the cut up and count treatment!

## What to do:

1. Invite children to find their talk partner and sit down in the circle next to them (see Talk partner, talk, p.20).

2. Introduce the puppet to the circle. Ask the children to introduce their partner to the circle.

3. Show the children the puppet's name written down on a strip of paper. Choose a child to come and count how many letters there are in the puppet's name.

4. Cut up the name into individual letters so they are easier to count and then stick them back down in the right order onto a strip of coloured card.

5. Ask the children to write their name using big letters so that they can be cut up and counted. Provide scissors for each pair of children and ask them to carefully cut their name up into individual letters. Can they stick them back together in the right order?

6. Go round the circle and find out how many letters each child has in their name. Who has got the longest name in the group?

7. Choose a 'tally master' to keep a tally of how many names have three, four, or more letters.

# Rhyme rings

Enjoying the sound of rhyme

## What you need:

- Whiteboards
- Whiteboard pens

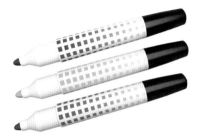

## Top tip ⭐

Children need freedom to play around with rhymes before they recognise them instantly. Don't worry if this results in some made up words!

### What's in it for the children?

Recognising rhymes is an important skill towards developing reading in young children.

### Taking it forward

- Play a game of 'Rhyming bells'. Choose one child to be the bell ringer. They sit in the middle of the circle with a hand bell. Share some nursery rhymes or poems with the children. Ask the bell ringer to ring the bell every time they hear a rhyming word.

- Let children write out some of the rhyme rings on a circular ring of paper and hang them up on display to remind the children of some rhyming words.

## What to do:

1. Invite children to sit in a circle next to their talk partner (see Talk partner, talk, p.20).

2. Start by singing some favourite nursery rhymes together such as 'Twinkle, Twinkle Little Star' and 'Hickory Dickory Dock'.

3. Ask the children to identify a pair of rhyming words from the rhymes with their talk partner and then share with the circle.

4. Give each pair a whiteboard and pen.

5. Explain that you are going to create a 'rhyme ring' around the circle. Choose a CVC word that has lots of potential rhymes, e.g. cat, van, dad, bag, and ask children to write a rhyming word on their whiteboard.

6. Go round the circle and ask children to say a rhyming word to create a 'rhyme ring'. How many rhymes are there in the ring?

7. Start by allowing nonsense words so long as they rhyme. Then stick to actual words and check children understand their meaning.

8. What is the longest rhyme ring they can make?

# Phonics games

Sharing phonics in the round

## What you need:

- Recording of sounds
- Selection of musical instruments
- Enough mats for one per child
- Set of cards with phonics or CVC words

## Top tip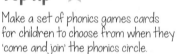

Make a set of phonics games cards for children to choose from when they 'come and join' the phonics circle.

## What to do:

1. Start by asking children to listen out for the initial letter that starts their name, 'Calling all the As!'. They can then join the circle. Go through the alphabet until all the children are seated.

2. Try some listening games. Record your own sounds for children to listen to and identify, or use a 'Listening lotto' game or pre-recorded set from the internet.

3. Try 'Whose sound is it anyway?' – a listening game using musical instruments. Place a selection of musical instruments inside the circle. Play a sound behind a screen. Choose a child to play the matching sound. Try a sequence of two or three sounds.

4. Play 'The magic sound' – a listening game using phonic sounds. Introduce one sound such as 's' or 'ee' as the 'magic sound'. Every time the children hear it they must slither like a snake, or jump into the air, etc. Start by humming quietly and then say the magic sound. Then say a sequence of other sounds and watch the children react when they hear the magic sound. Change the magic sound. Let the children think of new actions that correspond with each magic sound.

5. Play a game of 'Musical word-mats'. Make a circle of mats, one for each child, and place a word card on each mat. Ask children to stand behind a mat. Walk round the circle as the music plays. When it stops, everybody picks up the word off the mat nearest them and reads it out loud and then sits down on the mat. The fun starts when you gradually remove the mats so there aren't enough left for each child. Children who are 'out' can sit in the middle of the circle and watch. This also works as 'Musical chairs' if you have enough chairs for each child in the circle.

6. Play 'CVC dominoes'. Give each child a CVC word on a card, or make your own double dominoes by writing two CVC words on either end of a lolly stick or tongue depressor. Place the card on the floor in the middle of the circle. Invite the children to wave their card in the air if they can join it to the placed card. It has to start or finish with one of the same consonants. Or try a rhyming version where they can only place their card if the word rhymes.

**What's in it for the children?**

Learning phonics together through playing games is going to help all of the children gain confidence.

**Taking it forward**

- Encourage children to think up their own phonics games and provide resources for them to make cards, record sounds, and try out their ideas in the circle.

50 fantastic ideas for circle time

# Handwriting hints

Writing letters and words together

## What you need:

- Whiteboards
- Whiteboard pens

## Top tip ⭐

Many of these activities can be adapted to focus on a different Early Learning Goal. This can be changed to practise writing numbers or drawing patterns.

### What's in it for the children?

Once they have got past the fact that 'hand-writing' in this way is definitely ticklish, the children will enjoy trying to read what their partner is writing!

### Taking it forward

- If you use a particular handwriting scheme in your setting, try introducing activities at circle time. Children enjoy being able to see and share each other's ideas and efforts.

- This also works well as a maths game. Ask the children to choose a geometric shape such as a triangle, square or circle, and draw it on their partner's hand.

## What to do:

1. Ask children to sit in a circle next to their talk partner (see Talk partner, talk, p.20).

2. Sing the rhyme 'Round and Round the Garden' and invite them to take turns to trace a circle on each other's palms.

3. Ask them to choose a letter to trace on their partner's hand. Can their partner tell what it was without looking?

4. Can they write their name on each other's hands using just their finger?

5. Try writing some simple CVC words on their partner's hand for them to guess.

6. Play 'Chinese letters'. Try passing a letter round the circle by asking each child to write it on their partner's hand and pass it on. Does it stay the same all the way round the circle?

7. Try some 'Sky-writing'. Invite children to write letters and CVC words in the air.

8. Give each pair of children a whiteboard and pen. Ask them to take it in turns to write a letter and make some CVC words together. Hold their boards in the air to show the group.

# Super sentence search
Creating sentences in a circle

## What you need:

- 'Sentence stick' (any colourful stick)
- Whiteboards and pens

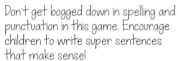

## Top tip ⭐

Don't get bogged down in spelling and punctuation in this game. Encourage children to write super sentences that make sense!

### What's in it for the children?

These games will help children to gain confidence in creating and writing simple sentences.

### Taking it forward

- Try joining the sentences into a story. Film the results.

- Play a game of 'Consequences'. Start by giving each child a piece of paper and ask them to write down a boy's name at the top and then fold down the paper over the writing. The next player adds a girl's name. Play continues with: where they met/what he said/what she said/what he did/ what she did, and ends with 'The consequence was…'.

## What to do:

1. Ask the children to sit in a circle next to their talk partners (see Talk partner, talk, p.20).

2. Talk about what makes a super sentence. Remind them about capital letters and full stops but emphasise that the sentence must make sense! Model some good examples but keep them short and simple.

3. Explain that in this sentence search game, the children only have to say one word.

4. Start off with 'I', 'Today' or a name and pass the 'sentence stick' to the next child.

5. When a sentence is completed, ask the next child to jump up and write a full stop in the air with the 'sentence stick'. This should encourage everybody to keep listening because they will all want a turn!

6. Write the completed sentences on a whiteboard for the children to see.

7. Repeat the game but ask all the children to talk to their partner and write their joint idea for the next word on a whiteboard and hold it up.

8. Try starting the sentence with the words 'Fortunately' or 'Unfortunately'.

# My grandmother went to market

Memory games using nouns and adjectives

## What you need:

- Shopping basket
- Cards with pictures and CVC words

## What to do:

1. Ask the children to sit in a circle and sing the alphabet song together to the tune of 'Twinkle, Twinkle Little Star'.

2. Start with an aural version of 'My grandmother went to market' and ask children to think of things for her to buy all starting with one initial letter such as 'b' or 's'. Go round the circle adding to her shopping basket. How long a list can the children recall?

3. Try the alphabet version. Each item has to start with the next letter of the alphabet (see Alphabet shopping, p.35).

4. Use cards with pictures and CVC words for children to read and add to the basket. Give each child in the circle a card or place a pile of cards face down in the middle.

5. You can choose to leave the cards face up to aid memory or make it harder by turning them over.

6. Play a game of 'The minister's cat'. Each child has to describe the 'minister's cat' with a different adjective going through the alphabet, so 'The minister's cat is an angry cat' and 'The minister's cat is a black cat', and so on.

## Top tip ⭐

Make sure there is an alphabet or phonics chart displayed on the wall of your setting for all the children to refer to.

### What's in it for the children?

Adding humour and drama into these memory games will enable children to remember more and have fun.

### Taking it forward

- Try the game with harder CCVC or CVCC words and no pictures!

- Place some props in the circle and a shawl, hat and basket for 'granny' to carry and encourage children to act out the game. Does this help the children to remember the sequence of items?

# A counting circle

Practise counting with friends

## What you need:

- **A puppet**

### What's in it for the children?

Working together in the counting circle will increase children's confidence in using numbers.

### Taking it forward

- Try some tricky questions such as, 'If we start at 14 and count in ones round the circle this way, what number will _____ say?'. Invite children to make up their own tricky questions.

- Make the counting order more random by playing 'Look at me'. Ask the children to stand up. The child who starts counting has to make eye contact with another child who steps forward and says the next number. They then make eye contact with another child who steps forward and continues the count.

## What to do:

1. Ask the children to come and sit in a circle so that they can see and hear each other. Use the 'Come and join us' song (see p.6). Change the last line to *Time to count*.

2. Introduce the counting puppet to the children.

3. Let the puppet start with the first number: 'one' and then count on round the circle in order.

4. Add an action so the child says their number and then has to jump up, sit down, spin round or clap their hands.

5. Try starting with a different number such as 10, 11, 12, etc. so the children can practise counting beyond 20.

6. Remind the children how many are here today. Can they count backwards from that number?

7. Play 'Buzz'. When you shout 'buzz!' the counting has to change direction around the circle!

8. Ask the children to sit next to their talk partner in the circle (see Talk partner, talk, p.20). Try counting in twos. After each number, a pair can jump up!

9. Practise counting in fives and tens to introduce multiplication.

# Roll the dice

Dice games in a circle

## What you need:

- Empty cube-shaped box
- Paper and pens
- Whiteboards and pens
- Whiteboard eraser

## Top tip ⭐

Encourage children not to shout out answers and give the child who rolled the dice a chance to answer!

### What's in it for the children?

Lots of practise counting spots on the dice will eventually enable children to be able to recall the number arrays without counting.

### Taking it forward

- Try a shape version of this game. Stick pictures of six different geometric shapes onto the faces the dice. How quickly can children recognise and name the shapes?

- Challenge more able children by putting simple number sentences onto the faces of the dice, using three or four different dice, or even including 100+ numbers.

## What to do:

1. Make a homemade dice with a small group of children by covering a box with plain paper and drawing the spots or pips in the traditional arrays.

2. Ask children to sit in a circle and take turns to roll the large dice back and forth to each other, allowing time for children to count the pips and call out the number.

3. Can they tell you the number without counting, just by recognising the arrangement of spots on the dice?

4. Write a list of numbers 1–6 on a whiteboard. Ask children to come and rub out the numbers as they are rolled.

5. Turn it into a team game with multiple different coloured dice. Which team can rub out all six numbers the quickest?

6. Change the dice to a numeral dice. Start with numbers 1–6 and then use numbers from 7–12 and 11–20 to practise recognition of double digit numbers.

7. Use two dice and ask the children to add the two numbers together. Make a list of the numbers 2–12 for children to rub out.

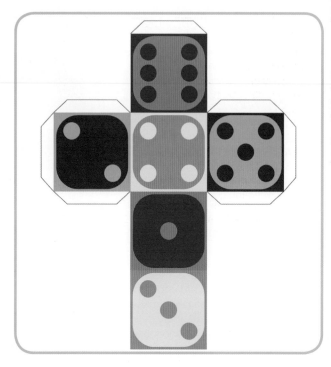

# Maths puddles

## Puzzles with puddles

## What you need:

- Scissors
- Blue paper or plastic
- Marker pen
- Sticky tack

### What's in it for the children?

Combining moving with maths is a great activity for children who prefer to learn kinaesthetically.

### Taking it forward

- Differentiate the activity by asking more able children to find the answers to trickier calculations.

- Use hula hoops instead of puddles. Try some number sentences. Place three hoops in the middle. Ask two children to stand in one, and three in the next. Make + and = signs using masking tape. How many children will there be in the answer hoop?

- Try a game of 'Countdown'. Split the circle into two semi-circles. Line up half of the puddles in order in front of one team and the other half in front of the second team. Ask each team to roll dice and count down that many puddles from the highest number. Use a counter or a child to jump down the line of puddles. The team that gets to the end first wins. This also works as an addition game starting with the lowest number.

## What to do:

1. Cut out some puddle shapes from blue paper or plastic and number them 0–10 or 11–20.

2. Invite the children to sit in a circle and place the puddles randomly on the floor in the middle of the circle using sticky tack.

3. Start by asking a child to jump onto one specific numbered puddle.

4. Invite the children to take turns jumping around the puddles in order, forwards and backwards, counting as they go.

5. Can they find the puddle that is one more or one less than a given number?

6. Shout out simple addition or subtraction facts for them to jump on the answer.

7. Ask children to take turns to call out numbers for others to find. Invite the puppet (see A counting circle, p.43) to join in calling numbers.

# Great shapes

Games to recognise shapes

## What you need:

- Long loop of string with one button threaded onto it
- Fabric bag
- Plastic shapes
- A puppet
- Masking tape

## What to do:

1. Make a giant circle on the carpet using a long loop of string with one button threaded onto it. Ask the children to sit around the edge in a circle and hold the string in front of them. Who has got the button?

2. Play a game of 'Pass the button'. Ask children to move the button on the string around the circle and sing *'Button, button, where are you? Here I am, here I am, in ____ hand'* to the tune of 'Tommy Thumb'.

3. Can the children spot where the button ended up? Ask for a volunteer to sit in the middle, close their eyes and try to work out where the button has gone.

4. Ask children to place the loop of string on the floor behind them and to sit inside the giant circle.

5. Pass round a fabric bag full of different plastic 2D shapes. Invite some children to put their hand in the bag, feel a shape, and without looking, identify it.

6. Ask the counting puppet to join in (see A counting circle, p.43). Help him/her to feel a shape, describe it and see if the children can identify it from the description, e.g. 'It has four sides that all feel the same'.

7. Make some big 'great shapes' on the carpet using masking tape – square, triangle, rectangle, diamond, etc.

8. Give each child a plastic shape to hold. Make sure they know the name of the different shapes.

9. Call out a shape and ask children with the same plastic shape to go and stand inside the 'great shape'.

10. If you shout out 'circle', they all have to stay sitting in the giant circle loop.

## Top tip

These games work well outside where you can use chalk instead of masking tape. Let the children add rocks and stones along the shapes to make some 'great rock shapes'.

### What's in it for the children?

Handling shapes and playing lots of different games will help children to become more familiar with their names and properties.

### Taking it forward

- Show the children how to change the shape of the loop of string from a circle into an oval, egg, sausage, and even a square or triangle. Is it harder to play 'Pass the button' in these shapes?

- Try putting 3D shapes in the fabric bag for children to guess. Can they name the different shapes – sphere, cone, cube, pyramid, etc. Encourage their use of mathematical language such as 'sides', 'faces', 'corners' etc.

# Wiggly worms

A tin of numbers, worms and maybe more!

## What you need:

- Card
- Pens
- A small tin or bucket

## Top tip ⭐

This is sure to be a popular game as it's so versatile; it's a good idea to laminate the cards before the children handle them!

### What's in it for the children?

Learning is always more fun if there is the chance of an opportunity to wiggle, move, curl up and hug each other.

### Taking it forward

- This game can be used to practise other maths skills or adapted for other areas of the curriculum: add shape cards to the mix; try colour recognition cards; write simple sums on the cards; or try phonics or CVC words to develop reading and literacy.

## What to do:

1. Make a set of number cards – use numbers 0–20 or any numbers that your children are learning. Include dice spot arrays as well as numerals.

2. Add some special cards: a wiggly worm (draw a cartoon-style worm), heart, and bird.

3. Place all the cards in the tin or bucket and invite children to join you in a circle to play.

4. Pass the tin around and ask each child to remove a card and tell the group what it says. Remind them that they can 'phone a friend' if they get stuck.

5. If the 'wiggly worm' card is drawn, all the children must stand up and 'wiggle' on the spot for a count of ten. Alternatively, the children can wriggle around the room so long as they are back to their spot on ten!

6. If the 'bird' card is drawn, all the children must curl up in a ball so the bird cannot eat them. This can also be used as an end card!

7. If the 'heart' card is drawn, invite the children to hug their neighbour.

8. At the end, collect the cards back by calling out numbers for children to return cards.

# Counting towers

Counting and team-building

## What you need:

- A puppet
- Paper plates
- Pens
- Basket
- Building bricks or wooden bricks
- Music
- Cardboard boxes and sugar paper
- A whistle

## Top tip ⭐

Try to ensure that all the children have a turn.

### What's in it for the children?

Working together cooperatively to build number towers and balance structures is a good team building exercise.

### Taking it forward

- Write large numbers on the homemade bricks and make it harder by asked the children to build the towers in order.
- Challenge the children to build a tower using only odd or even numbers.

## What to do:

1. Ask the children to come and join you in the counting circle. Use the 'Come and join us' song (see p.6).

2. Invite the puppet to join in the activity. He/she can bring along some of the equipment (see A counting circle, p.43).

3. Place some paper plates around the circle. Ask some children to go and write a different number on each plate. Start with 0–10.

4. Put a basket of building bricks or wooden bricks in the centre for children to access.

5. Ask the puppet to choose a plate and read the number. Use the 'Lolli-pot' (see Introduction, p.4) to choose pairs of children to fetch bricks and build a tower using the same number of bricks.

6. Play 'Musical towers'. Position the plates evenly around the circle.

7. Play some music as the children pass the plates around. When the music stops, the children holding the plates must put them down in front of them, read the number, fetch the matching number of bricks and build a tower. If the music starts up again before they've finished building, their efforts have to be abandoned.

8. Try 'Counting towers' in teams with homemade bricks that are harder to balance and build with. Try wrapping some junk boxes with sugar paper to make a variety of sizes of bricks. Blow the whistle and in two minutes see which team can build the tallest tower.

# What's the time?

Games using clocks and stopwatches

## What you need:

- Large plastic hoop
- Large whiteboard or paper and pen
- Clock hands cut from coloured foam
- Paper plates
- Marker pens
- Cardboard strips
- Split pins

## What to do:

1. Start singing 'Hickory Dickory Dock' and invite the children to join in, march around, form into a circle and use their voices and arms to do the 'tick tocks'!

2. Place a large plastic hoop on the floor in the middle of the circle on top of a large whiteboard or piece of paper. Write in the numbers 1–12 and cut out two giant clock 'hands'.

3. Choose a child to come out and make the clock say 'one o'clock' using the hands. Alternatively, children could draw on the hands.

4. Ask children to sit down next to their talk partner (see Talk partner, talk, p.20) and give each pair a paper plate, a marker pen, two strips of card, and a split pin.

5. Show them how to make a clock face using these materials.

6. Play 'What's the time?' – all the children have to make their mini-clocks match the one in the middle as quickly as they can and hold them up to show the group.

7. Invite a 'timekeeper' to call out a time for the other children to show on their clocks.

## Top tip ⭐

This can also be done with the hoop hung on top of a large whiteboard but this isn't as visible in the circle format.

### What's in it for the children?

Practical activities and games will reinforce children's understanding of telling time and reading clock faces.

### Taking it forward

- Try making a physical circle time clock. Choose 12 children to take a step into the circle and number them 1–12. Two more children have to lie on the floor and be the hour and minute hands! How quickly can they show the time you call out?

# DIY pie

## What you need:

- Images of pie charts
- Paper and coloured pens
- Mirrors
- String
- Coloured paper
- Camera

## Top tip

Be sensitive when collating any personal information for this activity so that children don't feel left out or excluded.

### What's in it for the children?

Practical maths activities are a great way to help children to understand handling and recording data.

### Taking it forward

- Talk in more detail about what the pie chart tells them. What is the most/least common eye colour in the group? If possible, relate the chart to simple fractions such as half and quarters.

- Ask the children to choose a different style of pie chart to create. Try to use their ideas. Look at other ways of recording information in graph form such as bar charts.

## What to do:

1. Invite the children to sit down in a circle so that everybody can see and hear each other.

2. Explain that you are going to make a special kind of pie – a pie chart. Show children images of pie charts.

3. First you need to decide on some information to collect. Start with eye colour. You could also try hair colour, type of pet, colour of car, etc.

4. Provide each child with a piece of paper with a large eye drawn on it and some coloured pens. Let children use mirrors and ask each other for help to decide on their eye colour. Colour in the picture.

5. Sort the children in the circle so that all the blue eyes sit together around the edge of their section of the circle, all the green eyes sit together, etc.

6. Find the centre point of the circle. Fasten pieces of string in the centre and stretch them out to divide the circle into slices for the different colours. Fill the sections with coloured paper.

7. Take photos of the pie chart to record the experience.

# Around the world

Travel to different countries

## What you need:

- Small carpet mat for each child
- A puppet
- World map or globe
- Suitcase or rucksack
- Different resources dependent on choice of destination!

## Top tip ⭐

This activity can be adapted to different countries. Choose places that are linked to your setting because of children's or adults' backgrounds or experiences.

**What's in it for the children?**

They will learn to recognise similarities and differences in relation to a variety of places and gain more of an understanding of the world.

**Taking it forward**

- Provide children with pictures cut out of magazines or travel guides and ask them to work with a partner to create a postcard from the chosen destination.

- Take the children on a magic carpet journey to a fantasy place inspired by a story or film and stimulate their imaginations. Ask the children to contribute their ideas of what the place might be like.

## What to do:

1. Make a circle of carpet mats and invite children to come and sit down. Explain that they are going to fly on their 'magic mats' to different parts of the world!

2. Pretend the mats are mini magic carpets, planes, trains, boats, or any other mode of transport.

3. Ask children to fasten their seat belts, and talk them through the journey. Use the puppet as a tour guide. Use a globe or world map to show the destination.

4. Fill a suitcase or rucksack with pictures and objects that represent the country, and share them with the children. Let children take turns to choose something from the bag to present to the circle.

5. Play music from the country when you arrive. Try some traditional dancing. Look at the country's flag. Show pictures online of significant buildings or landmarks. Try saying some words in different languages such as greetings or numbers.

6. Share food from the country around the circle at snack time. Open a cafe in the role-play corner serving food from around the world.

# Whatever the weather

## Comparing and sequencing

## What you need:

- Weather chart
- Empty plastic bottles
- Various fillings to represent weather, e.g. water, glycerine, pom-poms, rice, flitter, beads
- Basket
- Flat stones
- Acrylic paint

## Top tip ⭐

Looking at the day's weather together is a regular part of circle time. Try and make your way of doing it unique, entertaining and relevant to your children.

### What's in it for the children?

Weather is always being talked about so these activities will help children to observe their surroundings and notice changes that they can share.

### Taking it forward

- Relate the changes in weather to the different seasons and times of year.
- Try some weather experiments in the circle. Make a cloud in a jar, set up a rain gauge to measure rainfall, show the children a thermometer, or go outside on a sunny day and observe shadows.

## What to do:

1. Ask the children to sit in a circle and invite today's weather boy/girl to look out of the window and share what they can see.

2. Sing this weather song together:
   *Whatever the weather, whatever the weather,*
   *Whatever the weather, we share.*
   *Is it rainy or sunny, cloudy or fair,*
   *Snowy or blowy, we really don't care.*
   *Whatever the weather, we share.*

3. Use a weather chart to display the weather for the day.

4. Make a set of shakers with the children to encourage talk about the weather.

5. Fill six small plastic bottles with the following weather features: cloudy – water, glycerine, white pom-poms or polystyrene; rain – grey/black pom-poms, dry rice, blue glitter; snow – silver and white sequins, dry rice and glitter; sun – sand, one yellow pom-pom, yellow and orange beads; wind – small leaves; storm – water, glycerin, foam lightning flash, black pom-poms. Place the bottles in a basket and let the weather girl/boy choose one to shake and pass round the circle.

6. Make some weather stones by painting different weather features onto flat grey stones.

# Celebration circle

Celebrating cultural events together

## What you need:

- Recorded music or musical sound
- Props for birthday celebration or other significant event
- Calendar and materials for a birthday display

## What to do:

1. Use a specific piece of music or sound to signify that today's circle time is a celebration of a birthday or other special event. When children hear the music, they will know to come together for a 'celebration circle'.

2. Sing the 'Come and join us' song (see p.6) and change the last line to *Time to party* or *Happy birthday*.

3. Set up a birthday chair, and other props such as a sash or cape, birthday card or gift, cake to share, etc. Sing 'Happy Birthday'.

4. Make a birthday display showing the months of the year and children who have a birthday in each month. Use pictures of hot air balloons, candles, plants with a leaf for each child, and attach photos or self-portraits of each child.

5. Use the 'celebration circle' to share experiences of Christmas, Diwali, Hanukkah, Eid, Pancake day, Chinese New Year, Remembrance Day, Holi and other significant days.

6. Invite parents or visitors from the local community to join the 'celebration circle' and share their experiences of a festival or cultural tradition.

7. Talk about the children's experiences of celebrating festivals with their families. Sing songs, listen to music and share special food.

## Top tip ⭐

Circle time is the best way to get together and celebrate different cultural events – birthdays, festivals, anniversaries, and more. Make a calendar of appropriate events to celebrate at your setting.

### What's in it for the children?

Sharing and celebrating together is a good way to help children understand about similarities and differences between themselves and others.

### Taking it forward

- Play the 'Birthday Dash'. Call out a month of the year, and children whose birthdays are in that month, run around the outside of the circle and back to their spot.

# My poorly pet

Caring for animals

## What you need:

- Blindfold
- Visiting animal or pet
- Clipboards
- Paper
- Pencils
- Soft toy pet

## Top tip ⭐

If you have a visitor to talk to the children, it's a good idea to change the circle into a horseshoe shape so that nobody is behind the speaker!

## What's in it for the children?

The best way to learn about living things is to see them close up so these games will help children to observe animals.

## Taking it forward

- Make a pie chart to show the number of pets owned by the children (see DIY Pie p.51).

- Try some 'Magnetic fishing'. Cut out fish shapes from plastic or cardboard. Write numbers or letters on the underside. Attach paper clips. Let children take turns to go fishing using the magnetic fishing rod. Can they read their fish?

## What to do:

1. Ask the children to come and sit together in a circle so that they can all hear and see each other.

2. Play 'Who said that?'. Ask for a volunteer to sit in the middle of the circle wearing a blindfold. Point at a child to make an animal sound. Can the child in the middle guess who 'barked' or 'meowed'?

3. Play 'Animal Farm' (see p.28) and move like different animals.

4. Organise a visit from pets or other animals. Help children to make a list of questions to ask before the visit.

5. Give children clip boards, paper and pencils and invite them to sketch the pets.

6. Talk about pets that the children have at home. Sing 'My poorly pet' to the tune of 'Oh When the Saints':

   *My poorly pet,*
   *Must see the vet,*
   *My poorly pet must see the vet.*
   *He/She has hurt her _____.*
   *My poorly pet must see the vet.*

7. Pass a soft toy pet around the circle as you sing. The child holding it at the 'gap' can fill in the body part.

# Circle science
**Experimenting together**

## What you need:

- A puppet with safety goggles
- Shallow bowl
- Whole milk
- Food colouring
- Washing up liquid
- Tuff spot
- Brown paper
- Scissors
- Two plastic bottles
- White vinegar
- Red food colouring
- Baking soda
- Lava lamp
- Water
- Vegetable oil
- Effervescent antacid tablets, e.g. Alka-Seltzer®
- A light

## What to do:

1. Invite the children to come and sit in a small circle.

2. Introduce the puppet. Explain that he's wearing goggles because you are going to do some science experiments.

3. Create some 'Rainbow milk'. Place a shallow bowl in the middle of the circle and half fill it with whole milk.

4. Tell the children that they are going to add some food colouring. What do they think will happen?

5. Invite each child to come up, choose a colour and drop one drop into the milk. Talk about the different colours they can see.

6. Ask them what they think will happen if you add some washing up liquid or soap to the milk. Squirt some in and watch the swirling rainbow that results. How many different colours can they see now?

7. Try a 'Vinegar volcano'. Put a tuff spot in the middle of the circle. Make a cone out of brown paper and cut off the tip to create a hole. Use two small plastic bottles.

8. Pour some vinegar into one of the bottles and add some red food colouring and a squirt of washing up liquid.

9. Put three teaspoons of baking soda into the second bottle and place the cone over it in the tuff spot.

10. Pour the red liquid into the volcano and watch the eruption!

11. Make an easy 'Lava lamp'. Show the children a real lava lamp first, then pour water into a bottle until it's a quarter full. Then add vegetable oil until it's nearly full. Watch the two liquids separate.

12. Add some drops of food colouring and watch the blobs of colour fall down in the homemade lava lamp.

13. Ask the children what they predict will happen when you add the Alka-Seltzer® tablets? Break the tablet into quarters and add one to the bottle.

14. The blobs of colour should move up and down in a crazy fashion. Add another piece of tablet to keep the fun going. Shine a light through the bottle to get the full lava lamp glow.

### What's in it for the children?

Encourage children to make some predictions and observations as they share in the experiments.

### Taking it forward

- Find out more about the science behind these experiments to share with the children!

- Film the experiments so children can watch them over again and talk about what they think is happening.

### Top tip ⭐

These experiments work best with a small circle of children so that they can all be involved and see what is happening.

# Hands on
Group art activities

## What you need:

- Paper
- Shallow trays of paint
- Hand towels
- Scissors
- Large piece of cardboard
- Glue

## Top tip ⭐

*A quicker version of this activity is to make the hand prints straight onto the group picture to eliminate the cutting out!*

### What's in it for the children?

Seeing a picture emerge from their joint creative efforts is great to behold and will develop artistic confidence.

### Taking it forward

- Try a game of 'Passing prints'. Use a piece of A3 card, a tray of paint or a small ink pad or lipstick. Pass them round the circle inviting each child to add a hand print or fingerprint (or two) to the paper and see what work of art they can create together. Impose a time limit if necessary!

## What to do:

1. Ask children to sit down in a circle with plenty of room.

2. Place a piece of paper in front of each child. Pass round some small shallow trays of different coloured paint. Show children how to press their hand into the paint and make a hand print. Then pass round the hand towels to clean up!

3. Talk about colour, size, how the paint feels, and so on.

4. On the next day, or when the prints are dry, reconvene the circle and invite children to cut out their hand prints as carefully as possible.

5. Explain to the children that they are going to combine their prints into a group picture on a large piece of card. Choose which image to make. Here are some ideas:

   *Tree*: paint a brown trunk with branches. Let children glue on their hand prints as leaves.

   *Fish*: provide a large piece of blue paper or cardboard. Stick the handprints on like fishes swimming. Add eyes to the fish and paint in green weeds.

   *Rainbow*: draw the outline of a rainbow arch. Stick layers of coloured hands onto it to create a rainbow of hands.

# Sound pictures

## Using voices and instruments

## What you need:

- A selection of musical instruments, enough for one per child

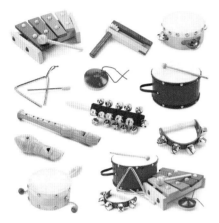

## Top tip ⭐

This activity works best if children have already had an opportunity to experiment with instrument sounds so they know what sounds they can make.

### What's in it for the children?

Working together to create sounds using voices, body percussion and instruments is a good way to represent their own ideas through music.

### Taking it forward

- Record and listen back to the sound pictures. How could they improve them? Which other sounds could they use? Paint a picture to go with the sounds.

- Ask children to choose a different inspiration for a sound picture, e.g. a starry night, a noisy city, a school playground.

## What to do:

1. Invite children to sit in a circle and listen carefully to the sounds around them.

2. Play 'Pass a sound around'. Invite children to take turns to make a vocal sound. Try tongue clicks, phonic sounds, animal sounds or words.

3. Repeat the game using body percussion, e.g. clap, tap, click, slap, stamp, etc.

4. Ask the children to make their sounds altogether.

5. Give out instruments so there is one for each child. Pass musical sounds around the circle, solo and altogether.

6. Create some sound effects. Invite children to make suggestions using vocal sounds, body percussion or musical instruments. Try footsteps, knock on door, alarm clock, owl, cat, insects, door creaking, wind, rain, thunder, etc.

7. Make a musical thunderstorm. Start with woodblocks/claves for raindrops. Add rainsticks and maracas as the rain pours. Use drums and tambourines for claps of thunder. Triangles and guiros make good lightning sounds.

8. Paint a jungle sound picture. In the background use voices to create a texture of sounds – monkeys, birds, insects in the hot jungle. In the foreground, start with slow footsteps through the undergrowth (stamping feet/tambourines), stop for a rest, cut away the big plants and vines ('swish'/guiros), fall over ('ouch!'/drum/cymbal), listen to the birds/insects.

# Art in the round

Different ways to be creative in a circle

## What you need:

- A piece of A4 paper on a clipboard for each child
- Pencil or crayon for each child
- Music
- Semi-circle shaped pieces of paper
- Wax crayons, oil pastels or chalks
- Giant piece of paper
- Small squeezy bottles full of paint

## What to do:

1. Ask the children to come and sit in a circle ready to create some art in the round.

2. Give each child a piece of paper on a clipboard and a pencil or crayon. Explain that they are going to make a 'chain drawing'.

3. While the music is playing in 10–20 second bursts, each child draws on the paper.

4. When the music stops they pass their picture onto the child on their left who adds to the picture.

5. Display the finished pictures for children to observe.

6. Play a game of 'Cartoon faces'. Talk about different cartoon characters and emojis. Provide each child with a circle drawn onto a piece of paper. Invite them to draw a cartoon self-portrait. Collect all the pictures and shuffle them. Can the children identify each other from their 'emojis'?

7. Give each child a small quarter or semi-circle shaped piece of paper. Show them how to colour them using oil pastels or wax crayons.

8. Encourage them to create patterns on their circle segment and to use at least two strong colours.

9. Ask the children to join their circle segments together with a partner or group to create a circle.

10. Stick them down as complete circles, next to each other, on a large piece of paper and display.

11. Show them a copy of Kandinsky's *Squares with Concentric Circles,* either before or after the activity.

12. Try creating a small group painting inspired by *Convergence* by Jackson Pollock. Place a huge piece of paper in the middle of the circle. Give each child a squeezy bottle with a different coloured paint and ask them to take turns to squeeze blobs, strings and patterns of paint onto the paper.

### What's in it for the children?

Lots of opportunities to be creative together and inspire each other to be artists in the round.

### Taking it forward

- Try a more formal version of chain drawing by playing 'Picture consequences'. Each child draws a head, folds down their picture, and passes it to the next child who draws the body and arms. The next child adds legs and feet. Finally, the 'creature' is revealed, named and shared with the circle.

- Set up a circle of easels, facing outwards and invite children to stand in a circle and paint pictures together. Invite them to paint self-portraits. Play some music and see if their paintings change.

# Conducting the orchestra
### Making music together

## What you need:

- A selection of different musical instruments, one for each child

: **Top tip** ⭐
:
: Practise stopping and starting
: instruments until children can stop
: straight away. Remind everybody to
: keep watching the conductor.

**What's in it for the children?**

This activity lets children explore the sounds and develop their control of different musical instruments.

**Taking it forward**

- Introduce conducting dynamics to the orchestra. Open hands wide apart indicates 'loud'. Open hands close together indicates 'quiet'.

- Ask children to sort instruments into groups by either materials, e.g. wood, skin (drums, etc.), metal, plastic, or how they are played, e.g. shake, tap, scrape. Give out instruments in these groups and ask conductors to visit each group and hear the different sounds they make. Which group of sounds do they like the best?

## What to do:

1. Invite the children to come and join the musical circle.

2. Sing the traditional song 'I am the Music Man' and encourage the children to mime each different instrument.

3. Play 'Who's the conductor of the orchestra?'. Ask for a volunteer to go outside while you choose the conductor of the orchestra. Everybody in the circle must copy the mime that the conductor does and change each time he/she does. Can the observer come back and identify who the conductor is?

4. Place a musical instrument in front of each child, in a random order.

5. Show them some simple conducting hand signals. Open hands, palms up indicates 'play your instruments'. Closed fists, palms down indicates 'stop'.

6. Practise starting and stopping all the instruments.

7. Invite children to take turns to be the conductor of the orchestra.

8. Ask them to go round and 'stop and start' individual instruments so they can compare and contrast the sounds.

# Rhythm games
Echo clapping and tapping

## What you need:

- Gathering drum
- Pairs of claves, enough for each child
- Two baskets

## Top tip ⭐

Most musical activities work brilliantly in the round. Everybody can see you and join in together without feeling too self-conscious.

### What's in it for the children?

They enjoy copying rhythms and changing them. As the children make music, they will be working together cooperatively.

### Taking it forward

- Try some rhythm patterns using body percussion, e.g. clap, tap, slap, stamp, click. Set up a repeated pattern using 'clap, clap, tap'. Can all the children in the circle copy the pattern over and over? Shout out 'Flipflop!' and change the pattern for them to copy.

## What to do:

1. Sit in a circle and invite the children to do some 'Echo clapping' by copying exactly what you clap. Start with simple four claps. Then try some more complicated rhythms.

2. Use word rhythms to help you such as 'pepperoni pizza' or 'fish finger sandwiches'.

3. Change it to quiet tapping with two fingers tapping on the palm of your hand. Mix and match clapping and tapping.

4. Invite children to take turns leading the echo clapping/tapping. Can they add a tasty word rhythm?

5. Place a gathering or large drum in the middle of the circle. Sing children's names to call them to sit around the drum.

6. Try some echo drumming on the gathering drum. Can the rest of the children in the circle drum the rhythm on their knees?

7. Pass round claves in two baskets. Invite each child to take a pair of matching claves and hold them on their knees, standing tall like candles.

8. Try some echo tapping using the claves. Divide into two or more clave teams and see which are best at echoing the rhythms accurately.

9. Choose children to be 'echo leaders' using the claves.

# The singing puppet

Singing favourite songs together

## What you need:

- A puppet with a moving mouth
- Large foam cube
- Marker pen
- A clave or 'bone'

## Top tip ⭐

With practice, the singing puppet can be used to encourage the children to sing together at all times of the nursery day.

**What's in it for the children?**

The children will enjoy singing songs and making music and experimenting with ways of changing songs.

**Taking it forward**

- Show the children a 'song bag' with cards or props referring to songs inside. Invite them to come and pick a 'clue' out of the bag and share the song with the circle.
- Set up a 'song mat' for children to perform a solo song of their choice to the group.

## What to do:

1. Use the puppet to invite the children to come and sit in the 'singing circle'.

2. Introduce the singing puppet to the children and let him/her demonstrate some singing skills.

3. Let children choose some songs for the puppet to sing. They can select the dynamics (loud/quiet), pitch (high/low), and tempo (fast/slow) as well.

4. Show the children a large dice made from a cube and scribe six favourite songs, one on each face.

5. Let the puppet roll the dice to see which song the group is going to sing.

6. Play 'Doggie, doggie'. Ask the puppet to choose a child to sit in the middle of the circle and be the 'doggie'.

7. The doggie hides his/her face while the bone is passed around the circle and all the children sing:

   *Doggie, doggie, where's your bone?*

   *Someone stole it from your home.*

   *Who stole my bone? (sung by the doggie)*

   *I stole your bone! (sung by the 'thief')*

8. The child holding the bone at the end of the song is the 'thief'!

9. Can the doggie identify the thief just from their singing voice?